CONTENT

Pinky At The Seaside

Chapter One

Pinky Spinks was staying with her friend Izzy who lived at the seaside. At this moment, Pinky was splashing about at the water's edge on the beach. She was too old to wear a bikini or a swimsuit but she had tucked her skirt into her knickers and was paddling up and down in the sea.

'Ooh, lovely !' she said out loud. She could feel the water oozing and the sand squelching between her pinky toes. Then, the tide would go out and she would wait for the water to roll in once more. The crests on the waves were like wild, white horses stampeding onto the soft sand !

Pinky had spent a super-duper week with her friend because there was so much to do at the seaside; particularly on the beach. Every morning there was a Punch and Judy Show. Then there were donkey rides and a large pool where you could catch crabs once the tide had gone out.

Pinky and Izzy had visited the theatre and cinema twice and had gone to the funfair on the seafront. They had tried the Scenic Railway, the Helter-Skelter and the scary Ghost Train. Woo-h ! That had made their hair stand on end !

This morning, Pinky had sat on one of the many deckchairs put out for parents while their children watched the Punch and Judy Show. Every day, there was a different play. Pinky thought they were really funny ! This morning Mr. Punch had a big stick with which he was practising hitting the floor so that later he could hit someone with the stick if he did not like them. Naughty Mr. Punch ! thought Pinky.

'That's the way to do it !' Mr. Punch kept saying over and over again in his squeaky voice as he hit the floor with his big stick. But behind Mr. Punch was a big, burly policeman !

'He's behind you !' the children kept shouting out to Mr. Punch. But every time Mr. Punch swung round to see who was there, the policeman bobbed out of sight.

Eventually, Mr. Punch swung around after another 'he's behind you,' and accidentally hit the policeman on the nose !

'Ouch !' cried the policeman. 'Right that's it ! We can't have you hitting people with that big stick. You just come along with me. I have got a nice, cosy prison cell waiting for you. That will teach you to go hitting good folk with a stick.'

How everybody laughed as Mr. Punch got dragged off the stage while Judy had arrived and waving goodbye, she said 'and good riddance!'

Pinky also liked to watch the children ride up and down the beach on the donkeys. There were four donkeys, Molly, Polly, Holly and Wally. Their owner Bill kept the donkeys on the beach in the summer season only taking them back to their stables in the evening.

Pinky loved the donkeys who were lovely ! Bill had made hats for each donkey. Wally had the biggest ears of all the donkeys so he had to have the biggest holes in his Mexican sombrero to allow his ears to poke through the holes. Molly and Polly had different kinds of hats with fruits and flowers on the brims of the hats. Holly, of course had a hat wreathed in holly with lots of red berries on it. The hats protected the donkeys heads and noses from the hot sun. Every day, Pinky brought the donkeys a bag of carrots for them and in return they nudged her with their noses to say a donkey thank you.

It was now lunchtime and all the families had dried themselves off after their swims and were going back to their hotels and guest houses for something to eat. Pinky went back to her place on the beach where she had spread out her pink beach towel. (it was in her nature to love anything that was pink !) She sat on the towel and dried her feet and then got out her picnic lunch that she had prepared. Bill came over to Pinky and asked if she would keep an eye on his donkeys while he went to do some shopping.

'Righty Ho !' replied Pinky. 'I'm going to eat my picnic lunch now so I won't be leaving the beach for some time. I will watch the donkeys for you.'

'Thank you so much !' Bill said. 'And, when I come back I will bring them some fresh water in the big cans that I keep. It is such a hot day and they have drunk all the water I brought with me this morning.' Bill loved his donkeys as much as he loved his family !

Pinky ate her lunch which consisted of ham and tomato sandwiches, some carrot cake and an apple followed by a long drink of fruit juice. Then, she laid down on her towel and covered her face with a big, floppy hat to keep the sun off. The beach was nearly empty but for a few people who were scattered here and there.

Pinky began to doze in the heat. Zzzzz ! She

began to snore softly. Suddenly, she was woken up by loud shouts. She pulled her hat off her face and sat up to see where the noise was coming from.

Two big boys aged about seventeen years old had come down to the beach, each holding a large spade and a bucket. They wanted to dig up some lug worms which were hidden deep in the wet sand for bait for a fishing trip. But, the tide was now in and almost up to the sea wall. Bill had been careful to leave his donkeys high up on the beach so they would not get wet.

Unable to dig for the lug worms the boys began to collect all the stones they could find and put them in their buckets. Pinky wondered what they wanted the stones for. It didn't take long for her to find out ! The boys sat down not far from the donkeys and began to throw stones at them.

'Go on Danny. See if you can hit them with a big handful of stones,' shouted one of the boys whose name was Pete.

'Better than that ! Get two handfuls of stones. You have got more of a chance of hitting them all at once !' laughed the other lad. 'Cor ! Listen to them braying. Ee ore ! Ee ore ! Stupid animals. Who would want to own one of them.

They are good for nothing they are !' said Danny scornfully.

The poor little donkeys were braying in pain and kicking up their legs to break free but they were tied too securely. Pinky was just going to tell the boys to stop being so cruel when Bill came back.

'Hey you !' he shouted as he came down the stairs onto the beach. 'What do you think you are doing?' Then, as the boys began to run away, taking their buckets and spades with them, Bill called after them,'If I catch you throwing stones at my donkeys again, I'll phone the police. You nasty devils. Devils ! that's what you are !' he shouted, at the same time shaking his fist at them.

Pinky got up and said, 'Don't worry ! They had only just got here, shouting and kicking up the sand. I was going to tell them to stop once they started throwing stones. Luckily, you got here just in time.'

'Well, yes. But what worries me is that I wasn't able to do all my shopping and the shops will be closed by the time I finish up here and take the donkeys back to their stables. I shall have to get the rest of my shopping tomorrow lunchtime and those nasty boys might come back again.' said Bill with an anxious look on his face.

'Well. If they do come back tomorrow, don't you worry ! I will think of something that I can do to deal with them,' said Pinky scornfully. And, she meant it! She had spent a lifetime curing children of their bad habits as well as grown-ups who didn't know how to behave properly. She was sure she could think of something that would show those spiteful boys that they shouldn't behave so badly.

Pinky went and sat back on her towel and watched the tide going back out. Gradually, people began to return to the beach in small groups. Soon, the little donkeys were trotting up and down the beach once more carrying children of all ages.

Meanwhile, Pinky wondered what she could do to show Danny and his friend Pete how spiteful they had been. Since she was on holiday she had not brought any of her magic powders or potions with her. Suddenly, she remembered that she had brought with her an old magic wand that had belonged to her father. She had brought it with her in case of any emergencies. Was this an emergency? Pinky thought it was ! She packed up her belongings and hurried back to Izzy's house. Izzy's holidays had come to an end and she had gone back to her job in the supermarket. Pinky intended to go home soon, as it wasn't so much fun being on holiday without Izzy with her.

When Pinky arrived back at Izzy's house, she went to her bedroom to look for the magic wand. It was lying at the bottom of her suitcase next to a big box of Boomerang Bon Bons. She had brought the Bon Bons as a present for Izzy but had forgotten all about them ! It was a fact that Pinky had created a new range of sweets called FUN SWEETS. The Bon Bons were very popular with the children in the village where she lived. You had to put the Boomerang Bon Bons in your mouth, then blow them out as hard as you could. The Bon Bons would zing and hum into the air then when they had gone as far as they could, they turned around and flew back again. The fun part came when you had to open your mouth and try to catch them. Some of the children who bought them had competitions to see who could send the Bon Bons the furthest !

Pinky went into Izzy's kitchen and made herself a cup of tea and helped herself to a sticky bun. Sticky buns were her favourite treat! She sat down in a comfy armchair and thought about how she could use the magic wand to save those poor donkeys from those spiteful boys.

Once she had refreshed herself with the tea and eaten the sticky bun she had a FANTABULOUS idea ! She picked up the box of Boomerang Bon Bons and took half of them and put them into a smaller box. The rest she kept for Izzy. She shut the lid of the small box and then waving the wand over the box she chanted in a deep, mysterious voice,

'Bon Bons you are,
Bon Bons you be,
You can be stones,
When I say,
One, Two, Three.'

Wow ! She thought. I hope this wand still works. After all, Dad had it all his life. I remember him using it when I was a little girl. 'Well !' she said out loud. 'There's nothing else I can do. I can't make magic potions in Izzy's house. It just has got to work !'

The next morning, Pinky went to the beach and again watched the Punch and Judy Show. This time a big crocodile appeared going snap ! snap! with his powerful jaws. He tried to snatch Punch and Judy's baby from his cot but Mr. Punch got out his big stick and whacked the crocodile on the nose saying, 'that's the way to do it, that's the way to do it.' The crocodile crawled away and Judy gave Punch a big kiss. Punch was a hero for a change !

At lunchtime, once again, the holiday makers left the beach to go and have some lunch. Bill came over to Pinky and said, 'I have to finish my shopping today. My wife is coming home from visiting her mother and I want to cook her a nice dinner. Can you keep an eye on my donkeys again? If those boys do come back to torment my donkeys, see if you can find a policeman and report them.'

'That's all right,' replied Pinky. 'You leave it to me to deal with them ! I have one or two tricks up my sleeve and believe me we won't need a policeman.' Bill wasn't at all convinced ! After all, Pinky wasn't very big but he had to get some shopping and there were no other people left on the beach to help.

Pinky had just sat down to unpack her lunch when the two boys showed up again. They had a bucket each already filled with stones so before they could start throwing them at the donkeys Pinky went over to them and said,

'Hello ! I made these sweets for a friend of mine but I made too many. Would you like some of them?' The two boys looked into the box of

Boomerang Bon Bons which were striped in many colours and looked very tasty.

'Oh okay. We will help you out. You don't want to waste them do you?' remarked Pete as he scooped out a handful of the sweets. Danny took out the rest of the sweets with two hands. Pinky noticed that neither boy said thank you.

Before she left the boys she explained that the sweets were FUN SWEETS ! You had to blow them from your mouth and when they returned to you, you had to catch them in your mouth again before you could eat them.

'That's why they are called Boomerang Bon Bons.' she told them.

'Oh okay. Sounds like fun. We'll have a go, won't we Dan?'

'Yeah ! See who can send them the furthest.' Danny said stuffing them into his mouth.

Pinky went and sat on her beach towel by the sea wall and watched both boys blowing out a mouthful of the sweets. The sweets travelled quite a way out then turned and zing ! zing ! they flew back to the boys. Just then Pinky said loudly,' ONE, TWO, THREE !'

The sweets were no longer Bon Bons, they were hard little stones. They hit the boys hard on their ears, arms, legs and bottoms.

'Ouch ! Ouch !' cried Danny. 'These sweets really hurt !'

'Ooh ! Ooh ! ' groaned Pete in agony. 'They aren't sweets are they? They are stones. How did they change from sweets to stones? Quick ! Let's leg it ! We have to get away. Hurry !' As the boys ran up the beach, the stones followed them, stinging them all over their bodies.

'That just serves you right !' said Pinky out loud. ' Now you know how much you hurt the donkeys, don't you? Well ! I don't think you will be doing it again !'

Just then Bill turned up holding two bags full of food and other items.

'Is everything all right here ?' he asked. 'Did those boys turn up again?'

'Well, they did.' answered Pinky. 'But I soon sorted them out. I don't think they will be back again.'

Bill looked at Pinky in amazement. After all Pinky was a chubby old lady but not very tall and certainly not as strong as the boys.

'Well !' remarked Bill. 'I hope you are right. I don't need to get any more shopping this week. Next time, I'll try and find a policeman if they come back. You are on holiday aren't you? So you won't be here much longer.'

'Yes, that's true. My friend I have stayed with has gone back to work so I think I will go home on the bus tomorrow. But, I have had a lovely holiday and I am so glad I could help you.'

Pinky had no intention of telling Bill about her magic because it was a secret ! Pinky was descended from a long line of magicians and wizards and they never told ANYONE about their magic although Pinky had on occasion admitted to making a magic wish !

Pinky packed up her beach things and went back to Izzy's house. Once there she made up her mind she would go home that day. After all, she was beginning to miss her little cottage and the village where she lived. She packed her holiday things and leaving a little note for Izzy, some photos of them together on holiday and the box of Boomerang Bon Bons she went to the bus station. She could not wait to get back home now and what would she do when she got home? Why, make more sweets and practise her magic of course !

Busy Bees

Chapter Two

Every week Pinky's neighbour and friend Queenie Green would come to Pinky's cottage and they would sit and chat about what was going on in the village and what they had read about in the local newspaper. Pinky would make a pot of tea, (her favourite pot with the pink roses on it) and make a scrumptious cake. Sometimes, Pinky made lemon drizzle cake, sometimes carrot cake but more often a big, pink, iced sponge cake as she loved anything that was pink! In return, Queenie always brought a jar of honey for Pinky because Queenie kept bees in her back garden. She had four hives which had very busy bees in them. Queenie grew lots of pretty flowers in her garden which was why the honey had such a lovely flavour.

Pinky used the honey for her sweets, in particular her 'Sunny Soothers'. These sweets were lovely for anyone with a sore mouth or for babies with sore gums when their first teeth were coming through. Pinky put some magic soothing potion into the sweets which melted in the mouth straight away.

Pinky and Queenie always met on a half day when Pinky's shop was closed and that half day was always on a Thursday afternoon. Today, she had made a strawberry sponge cake. It had layers of cream and strawberry jam finished with cream on top in which Pinky had stuck some fresh strawberries.

'Mm !' declared Pinky. 'I think this is the best cake I have ever made. I can't wait to eat it ! I hope Queenie gets here soon. I'll go and put the kettle on the stove and make the tea. I'm sure she will be here any moment now.'

Just then, just as Pinky had predicted, there was a knock on the door and Pinky went to open it.

'Hello Pinky !' said Queenie smiling. 'I hope I am not late. Ooh ! What a lovely smell coming from your kitchen. What cake have you made today for us?'

'It's a strawberry sponge.' announced Pinky proudly. 'You've got a good nose Queenie, haven't you?'

'Ooh lovely ! ' exclaimed Queenie, clapping her hands together. 'I love strawberries. I can't wait to eat it.'

'Nor me !' replied Pinky and giggling together like two little school girls they went into Pinky's parlour. Queenie sat in one of the comfy armchairs while Pinky poured the tea, cut two huge slices of the cake then putting these on a small table Pinky sat in the other armchair.

They were halfway through eating the delicious cake when Queenie said with her mouth half full and in a very doleful tone,

'Guess what Pinky ! I could not bring you any honey today because someone has been stealing my honey. I don't know who the thief is and I don't know how to stop him or her.'

'Really?' replied Pinky in a surprised manner. 'Well, that's just awful. I rely on your honey to put into some of my sweets.'

'Yes and it also means I have no honey to sell so I'm a bit short of money now. The honey money tops up my weekly shopping money,' remarked Queenie. 'I just don't know what to do about it. Whoever it is must come at night because I can never catch the person who is stealing it.'

'Well !' said Pinky, pondering the matter. 'If I come to you one evening we could take it in turns to watch through the windows overlooking your back garden. The nets covering the window are quite thick and if we keep the lights off, the person stealing the honey won't be able to see us.'

'Cool !' said Queenie. 'That's a really good idea. What about this evening. Are you free tonight?'

'Well, I'm not out on a date if that's what you mean,' giggled Pinky (Of course she was only joking as Pinky was a very old lady) In fact she had no idea how old she was !

'Oh, goody !' replied Queenie. 'If you can come to my house once it gets dark we can take it in turns to watch out.'

'Okey, dokey.' answered Pinky, nodding her head in agreement. 'Let's do it.'

Pinky and Queenie chatted together for about half an hour then played some games of dominoes, snakes and ladders and ludo. Then, Queenie went home to cook her dinner. Pinky cleared away the tea things and cooked a nice chicken pie, potatoes and peas for her own dinner. She put some of the chicken into her cat Sydney's dish. Sydney loved fish best of all but chicken made a nice change for him.

Once it started to get dark, Pinky slipped next door to Queenie's house and the two friends took it in turn to look out of the window into Queenie's back garden. Pinky grinned to herself when she heard Queenie snoring,

'ZZZzz, ZZZzz.' Queenie's snores almost sent Pinky to sleep but just as she was about to doze off, someone in the back garden knocked the dustbin lid off the dustbin. Pinky nudged Queenie at once and Queenie woke with a start.

'Wassup ? Wassup?' Queenie mumbled, sitting up straight.

'Ssh,' whispered Pinky. 'Someone is out there in the garden. Quick, go and fetch a torch. Let's see who the culprit is.'

Queenie grabbed a torch from the cupboard under the stairs and the two friends crept towards the back door. Suddenly, 'yowl, meow, meow.' It was Sydney. He had jumped off the fence between Pinky and Queenie's gardens and made a lot of noise doing it !. Immediately, whoever had been in Queenie's garden sprang over the bottom fence and escaped. Pinky and Queenie went out into the garden and shone the torch all around and then on the ground.

'Look !' said Queenie. 'Here's a can that bee keepers puff out smoke from to make the bees sleepy while they take the honey from the hive. This person knows a lot about bees. He or she knows not to get stung. What shall we do?'

'Well ! We are not giving in that's for sure !' replied Pinky. 'Leave it to me. I'll think of something. I'll come again at the same time tomorrow night and the next time we will catch the thief !'

Pinky was well known for her good ideas but she never told anybody about her magic, not even her best friend Queenie. People knew she could make magic wishes but that was all !.

Promising Queenie that she would definitely come back the next night, Pinky went home. She made herself a cup of tea and cut another slice of the delicious strawberry cake and pondered what to do about the honey thief. Then she had an AMAZING idea. She would coat the top of the hives with purple colouring which she usually used to coat her Parma Violet sweets. Whoever was pulling out the trays from the hives with the honey on them would accidentally get the purple colouring on their fingers.

Then, Pinky and Queenie would go around the village and knock on every door. There was to be a dog show soon on the village green and Pinky and Queenie had volunteered to take the leaflets about the dog show to every house. It was a perfect opportunity to find the thief. Feeling very pleased with herself, Pinky went up to bed and was soon dreaming of new names for her scrumptious sweets !

The next morning, Pinky went next door to Queenie's house and told her about her FANTASTIC idea. Queenie agreed it was a jolly good plan and bound to work. Pinky went back and fetched the purple colouring and coated the tops of the hives with it. The colouring could be seen in the day but not at night !

That night the two friends waited patiently and soon enough they heard someone creeping around in Queenie's garden. Thinking they might be able to catch the thief themselves they rushed out into the garden. But, it was too late. The thief had escaped once more. This time they shone the torch onto the ground and found a big jar partly full of honey.

'We must have frightened the thief when we opened the back door.' commented Queenie.

'Yes, but it doesn't matter. Tomorrow we will start taking the leaflets around the village when everyone gets home from work. Then, we will find out who has got purple colouring on their fingers and we can go to the police station and tell the police.' said Pinky excitedly. Then nudging Queenie, she giggled. 'Perhaps the police will ask us to join the police force. We make good detectives don't we?'

BUT, Queenie and Pinky did not need to take

the leaflets about the dog show around the village yet because the next morning a door-to-door salesman came into Pinky's shop.

'I'm a bee keeper and I live locally.' he said. 'Would you like to buy some of this lovely honey? AND, he put six jars of honey on the counter of Pinky's shop WITH PURPLE FINGERS ! Pinky stared in amazement at the jars of honey and the man's hands.

'Just a minute !' she said. 'I'll just go out to my store room and see if I need any honey. I'll be back in a jiffy !' Instead, Pinky went out into her garden and climbed over the fence into Queenie's garden. Queenie was pegging out some washing on the clothes line.

'Guess what Queenie !' exclaimed Pinky in an excited voice. 'There's a man in my shop with purple fingers trying to sell me some jars of honey. Quick ! Get on your bike and go to the police station while I try to keep him in my shop!'

Pinky climbed back over the fence once more and went into her shop. She checked the till to make sure the man had not taken any money from it ! Normally, he might have done, but the thief was afraid he might leave purple marks on the till and instead had waited patiently for

Pinky's return.

'I've checked my honey store and I think I could buy two of your jars of honey,' Pinky said to the man. Then, she started to tell the man how she used honey for the sweets that she made. She started to count the different sweets on her fingers very slowly.

'Well ! There's Honey Hoops, Honey Soothers, Crunchy Honey Hearts, Happy Honey Humbugs, Happy.....'

'Yes. Yes,' said the man interrupting Pinky. 'Very interesting I must say. Just give me the money for the honey Mrs. Spinks. I still need to sell the other jars. The honey is £1 a jar, okay?'

Just then the village policeman P.C. Probyn came in with Queenie who had told him all about the trap Pinky had set for the thief on the way to Pinky's shop.

'Right you. You 'orrible man !' said P.C. Probyn, pulling the man's arms back and putting handcuffs on his wrists. 'You just come back to the police station with me. I want a good explanation of 'ow you acquired this 'ere honey and 'ow you got your 'orrible purple fingers. !'

The thief protested that he was a bee keeper but P.C. Probyn was having none of it ! By now a police car had arrived outside Pinky's shop and the thief was put into the car and taken to the police station.

Immediately, there was a rush of customers to Pinky's shop. They all wanted to buy some sweets but even more they wanted to know why there had been a police car outside Pinky's shop!

Pinky and Queenie told everybody about the stolen honey and the next day a reporter from the local newspaper came to Pinky's shop to write up what had happened.

THE DAY AFTER THAT there was a picture of Pinky and Queenie on the front page of the local newspaper with the story about the stolen honey. Once again Pinky was famous ! But not just famous because everybody in the village talked about the stolen honey and agreed that Pinky was not only a heroine for catching the thief, but a heroine WHO MADE SCRUMPTIOUS SWEETS !

Fibbing Fiona and the Needy Nougat.

Chapter Three

Fiona had come to stay with her Aunty Beth and Uncle Barry for a few weeks because her mother was in hospital and there was nobody else to take care of her. Fiona was a happy, lively little girl but she told so many fibs ! She so wanted to make lots of friends that she told lots of lies to make people like her.

When Fiona came into Pinky's sweet shop for the first time, immediately she said 'hello' to some other little girls who were waiting in a queue to buy some sweets.

'Hi there !' Fiona said smiling at the girls. 'You don't know me but I am staying with my aunt and uncle for a little while. Would you like to come over to our house and then play rounders on the green? Our house is the first one as you pass the shops and it overlooks the green. My aunty will bring us out some lemonade and ice lollies when she sees us playing rounders. What do you think? By the way, my name is Fiona. What's yours?'

'I'm Amy, this is Laura and that's Cara,' replied the tallest of the girls. 'What do you think?' she asked her friends. 'Do you want to play rounders?' Laura and Cara nodded their heads.

'Yes. I would like that and we hadn't planned anything special for this afternoon, had we?' Laura said eagerly.

'Okay ! Well, that's settled then.' Cara said. 'We'll meet up at 2.00 o'clock after lunch. Don't forget to put on some shorts and trainers.'

'Oh good !' Fiona said. 'Of course my aunt and uncle's house is only small compared to my Mum and Dad's castle.'

'Castle ! You live in a castle !' exclaimed Amy. 'Goodness me ! You must be very rich. Is it a big castle?

'Oh yes. We are very rich. Our castle is huge. It's got turrets too and a long winding drive down to the road. You can't see it from the road. We've got a swimming pool, tennis courts and some stables with six horses and ponies too.' Fiona said, letting her imagination run away with her.

'Wow !' How lucky you are ! I would love to live somewhere like that.' said Cara.

'Well, let's see how we all get on. Then if you like I will write to my Mum and Dad and ask if you three could come and stay for a bit. You can ride the ponies if you like. Of course if you want to.' Fiona added hastily.

'Gosh ! Want to ! I will be first in the queue don't you worry about that !' commented Laura, laughing with her two friends. 'What do you think girls?'

'Ooh yes ! It would be great if your Mum and Dad would let the three of us visit together. Thank you so much Fiona ! Well, we will see you on the village green at 2.00 o'clock. Will you bring the rounders equipment?'

'Yes. Our house is the nearest so that makes sense. I'll go and tell my Aunty we will be playing rounders outside and we will want some lemonade and ice lollies when we get thirsty. See you all later then.'

Amy, Laura and Cara bought their sweets and left the shop leaving Fiona to look at all the kinds of sweets that Pinky had made.

'What would you like to buy? There's plenty to choose from. How about some Fruity Foo Foos or some Whizzing Whoppers?' asked Pinky.

'I haven't got much money. What are the cheapest sweets you have got Mrs. Spinks?' Fiona said, looking a bit miserable.

'There's only a few really cheap sweets,'

answered Pinky. 'You see most of my sweets have special ingredients. How about some Needy Nougat? It comes in lots of flavours. You can have vanilla and peach flavour or vanilla with other flavours like orange, lemon and apricot.'

'Why is it called Needy Nougat?' laughed Fiona. 'Your sweets have very funny names don't they?'

'Well, yes they do but that's why people like them. You can't buy these sweets I make anywhere else, they are unique. Needy Nougat is called that because as soon as you have eaten a bar of it, you need to eat another one straight away because it is so delicious.' replied Pinky.

'Oh, they all sound very tasty. I'll have two bars of the vanilla and peach flavour please,' Fiona said as she began to count out her money. 'Oh, I've only got fifty pence and it's got to last until Saturday. Mummy is a bit short of money this week. Perhaps I had better just buy one bar. Can you break it into small pieces. I will eat just a few bits at a time. Like that I can make it last.'

Pinky was astonished. Being a bit short of money didn't tally with what Fiona had told Amy, Laura and Cara. That she lived in a castle and her family was very rich ! Obviously Fiona didn't realise that I heard everything that she said to the other girls, thought Pinky. She took a Needy Nougat bar and broke it into small pieces with a little hammer. Then she put the nougat into a little plastic bag decorated with pictures of peaches and handed it to Fiona.

'There you are. That's twenty-five pence please.' Pinky said. Fiona thanked Pinky and left the shop. 'Well !' Pinky said out loud. 'There's nothing wrong with her manners. Also, she seems to be a happy little girl. Perhaps she really does live in a castle.'

Pinky turned the shop sign to 'closed' and went into her kitchen where she made some cheese on toast and a big pot of tea so that she could have several cups of it. (Yes, you are right! It was her favourite, old teapot with the big, pink roses on it !) Pinky ate her lunch slowly while she thought about what Fiona had said. If she was fibbing about living in a castle and being rich it was a naughty thing to do. It was giving false hope to three little girls who believed that Fiona was telling the truth and would be looking forward to staying in Fiona's castle home.

Now Pinky knew everybody in the village because everyone loved her superlicious, so delicious yummy, scrummy sweets !. So, Pinky decided to visit Fiona' s Aunty Beth while the girls were playing rounders to see if she could find out the truth. Telling fibs was no way to make friends. 'You had to be honest with your friends didn't you? Yes, you do !' Pinky said out loud. Looking at the kitchen clock which showed the time as a quarter past two, Pinky fetched her best jacket and locked the shop door. Then she made her way to Fiona's aunt and uncle's house.

Pinky crossed the green and as she passed the four little girls, she noticed that some of their school friends had joined them and the game of rounders was going well. There were plenty of players to take it in turns to bat, bowl and be out on the field to catch the ball.

Pinky knocked at Mr. and Mrs Barfield's front door and heard footsteps hurrying along the hall. In no time at all, Beth Barfield opened the door and exclaimed in surprise, 'Pinky ! How nice to see you. How have you been?'

'I'm very well, thank you,' replied Pinky. 'I just thought I would drop by and give you a leaflet about my latest sweets. I have created a new range of sweets which I am calling Fun Sweets. They are very popular already. Although, I expect you and Barry still prefer a box of Chewy Chocs don't you?'

'Yes, we do !' laughed Beth. 'But we only eat them on a Saturday evening as a treat ! Otherwise we would get too fat ! Really, I love them so much I could eat them all day. But do come in Pinky and we will have a nice cup of tea together. Barry is out playing bowls with his friends.'

Beth made some tea and fetched some biscuits. She and Pinky sat in the front lounge and now and then they glanced out of the front window to see how the game of rounders was progressing.

'Fiona has come to stay for a few weeks.' said Beth. 'I'm afraid her mother is in hospital waiting for an operation. She is quite poorly. Sadly, Fiona has no father now. He died when she was a little girl.'

'Still,' said Pinky. 'I expect Fiona has a new father now doesn't she ? So, they are quite well off.'

'Oh no !' exclaimed Beth. 'Fiona's mother did not get married again or get another partner. Fiona's mother works very hard cleaning offices. They don't have much money which is why I try to spoil Fiona while she is here. I try to make her favourite dinners, desserts and cakes and I intend to take her to the cinema as often as I can to see her favourite films.'

'That's very kind of you,' said Pinky. 'I am sure Fiona will appreciate that. But oh look ! Fiona has bowled the ball too hard and it's smashed through the baker's window. I had better go out and see if I can smooth things over. It is time for me to leave anyway. Thank you so much for the tea and biscuits Beth. I will see you again quite soon I hope.' 'Oh, that's fine. It was so nice to chat with you Pinky. I will see you again soon when I come to buy another box of Chewy Chocs. My mouth is watering already so it won't be long !' laughed Beth as she opened the front door to let Pinky out.

Pinky hurried next door to the baker's only to find Fiona was already in the shop explaining what had happened to the baker, Mr Bentham.

'I am so sorry Mr. Bentham !' Fiona said. 'Some of my friends are a bit too rowdy and one of them threw the ball too hard. I will tell them all they must make a small donation to cover the cost of replacing your window. Will that be all right?'

'Well ! I suppose it will have to be !' replied Mr. Bentham irritably. 'But it will have to be mended today. I will pay for it and you can collect all the money from your friends and bring it to me when you have it all.'

'Oh, thank you Mr. Bentham !' answered Fiona. 'I'll go and tell the others at once !'

Pinky was shocked ! She had seen Fiona bowl the ball that had broken the window but Fiona had put the blame on somebody else ! Pinky followed Fiona out of the shop and as she passed the group of children she heard Fiona say,

'The baker is really angry. He said you have all got to put in enough money to replace the broken window. That will be £5 each. So, if you haven't got that much with you, you must go home and get it !'

'Well ! That's not fair ! You bowled the ball that broke the window !' retorted Laura. 'Surely, you should pay to have it mended. AND your family is rich and we aren't. In fact none of our parents are rich and they will be really cross about having to pay that amount of money.'

'Well, it can't be helped ! The baker said if you don't pay the money today he won't serve your parents any more. If they want any bread or cakes they will have to go into town to buy them.'

FIONA'S FIBS TOOK PINKY'S BREATH AWAY !

'Goodness, gracious me !' exclaimed Pinky as she walked back home. 'I have never heard anyone tell such dreadful lies to get themselves out of trouble. This is a matter I am going to have to sort out as soon as possible.'

When she returned to her shop, Pinky stood behind the counter but she did not really want to open the shop again. She was too bothered about Fiona's dreadful fibs and what could be done to help. For it was a fact that the truth will out and Fiona would be so unpopular when people found out how she had lied.

Suddenly she had a SUPER-DUPER idea ! She took one of the Needy Nougat bars and taking it in to her store room where she kept her magic potions and powders, she unwrapped the nougat bar and coated it with a very special magic liquid. A very special magic liquid indeed ! The liquid was colourless so it could not be seen when the nougat bar was unwrapped.

Pinky looked over to the village green and saw that all the children had gone home to get the money to pay for the broken window of the bakery. Pinky hurried across the green to Mr. and Mrs. Barfield's house. She knocked on the

door and to her surprise, Fiona opened the door.
'Oh, hello Fiona !' said Pinky. 'I was just telling your Aunty Beth about some of the new sweets I have created. Needy Nougat bars are a new creation too. Your Aunty Beth told me she will be taking you to the cinema soon. I thought you could take some nougat bars with you. The vanilla and lemon flavour one is for you and the apricot and peach flavoured ones are for your aunt and uncle. So, here you are. They are a gift from me,' said Pinky, handing the sweets to Fiona.
'Oh, thank you Mrs. Spinks. That's really kind of you. I'll go and give them to Aunty Beth for when we go to see a film.'
While Pinky walked slowly home, Fiona took the nougat bars to her Aunty who was busy in the kitchen.
'Oh, that's all right Fiona. You can eat them all. Your uncle and I don't like nougat but Pinky would not have known that. It was very kind of her to bring them. It's teatime soon but you can eat one bar now and keep the rest for when we visit the cinema.' said Aunty Beth.
'Oh goody !' exclaimed Fiona. 'I'll eat the lemon and vanilla one now as I have already tried the peach flavoured one and apricot flavour will

be similar to that.' Saying this, Fiona curled up on the settee in the lounge and began to read a really exciting adventure story. She ate the nougat bar quite quickly but then found that she just could not concentrate on her book. She felt an incredible urge to do something. This urge was driving her, driving her to tell her aunty the truth about the broken window. She went into the kitchen where her aunty was preparing the tea.

'Aunty ! Aunty !' said Fiona. 'I need to tell you something. I need to tell you something right now. I do hope you won't be cross !'

AND with that, Fiona blurted out the truth about the broken window. Suddenly, she felt much better. So much better !

'Do you mean to tell me Fiona,' Aunty Beth said crossly. 'That all those children have gone home to ask their parents for £5 to pay for a window that YOU broke !'

'Yes and I am sorry, Aunty. I am sorry and ashamed. If you could pay for the broken window to be mended, I will do any jobs you want done. I promise I won't turn down any job, no matter how difficult it might be. I don't know why I tell fibs. I just sort of got into the habit of telling lies. I will try really hard to be truthful in future.' Fiona said, looking very downcast.

'Goodness me, Fiona. It's going to take a lot of money to pay for that window to be mended. So, yes I think that means you will be doing a lot of jobs for me until it's time for you to go home!' Poor Aunty Beth went to a tin on the dresser where she kept her shopping money and took all of it to Mr. Bentham's bakery to see how much the new window would cost. The new window was in place but it cost all the money in Aunty Beth's tin!

'You can tell all the children who are bringing money for the replacement window to take it home again.' Aunty Beth told the baker. 'Tell them please that the window is paid for.' But Aunty Beth was too ashamed of Fiona to tell the baker who had really broken the window.

Well, Fiona was kept busy for the rest of the two weeks she stayed with her Aunty Beth and Uncle Barry. She swept and mopped the floors, cleaned windows, peeled the potatoes for dinner and did the shopping. She didn't have time to play with the new friends she had made so didn't have to ask them to the castle she had pretended to live in ! Still, Aunty Beth did take Fiona to the cinema because she had promised to and she always kept her promises even though Fiona didn't really deserve to go. Fiona probably would never had told the truth if she had not eaten the magic nougat bar !

After two weeks, Fiona's mother was well enough to come out of hospital. The Fiona who returned home was a very different little girl. Still a happy little girl but one who knew that TELLING LIES ABOUT HERSELF WOULD NOT WIN HER ANY FRIENDS !

The Unwanted Dog

Chapter Four

The village committee was meeting in the village hall to discuss the forthcoming dog show which was to be held on the village green. There were so many dogs in the village that someone suggested it would be a good idea to have a dog show to raise some funds for repairs to the village church.

The reason there were a lot of dogs in the village is because a trader had once come to the village's Saturday Market to sell his puppies. However, the puppies were not well treated and Pinky had helped them to escape. These puppies had found homes with the people living in the village and had grown into all sorts of dogs. There were huge ones, small ones, short-haired ones, fluffy ones, curly tail ones and long-tailed ones; in fact all sorts !

The village committee decided that the dog show would have four main categories for showing the dogs and they were;

1. The dog with the waggiest tail.
2. Performer of the best tricks.
3. The prettiest dog.

4. The most handsome dog.

Pinky did not have a dog, only Sydney her cat but she loved all animals and the committee had voted that she should be a judge as well as the head person of the committee, Mrs. Sproggins.

Feeling very pleased with themselves now the decisions had been made about the dog show, the committee members were just about to leave when P.C. Probyn knocked at the door and then came in with a very scruffy dog in his arms. He put the dog down on the floor and everyone could see that the dog was very thin, his bones showing through his rough coat. He was filthy and stood there shivering and shaking all over. Everybody crowded around the dog.

'Just look at the state of this poor dog !' exclaimed P.C. Probyn. 'I was on patrol walking past those tumbledown old cottages that back onto the river when I heard a dog whimpering. I checked the back doors of each cottage and they were all empty. But I found this dog in the last cottage. The people who had rented the cottage had moved out and left this poor dog behind, There were no dog bowls with any water or food in either.'

'Oh !' exclaimed Pinky. 'So nobody knows how long it has been since he had anything to eat or drink. By the look of him, my guess is that it was a long time ago ! Goodness, gracious me, he's like a bag of bones !'

The dog's head was drooping low and his tail was down between his legs. His coat was dull and dirty and he suddenly collapsed on the floor, he was unable to stand any longer. Everybody felt really sorry for him.

'What are you going to do with him then?' asked Mrs. Sproggins.

'I'm going to put him in the dog pound for unwanted dogs in the police station yard. He's in such a bad way I don't think there is much hope for him, poor thing.' replied P.C. Probyn.

The committee members nodded their heads. They all thought the dog was too far gone to be nursed back to health. Just then Pinky looked over at little Mrs. Lovebody who was standing on the edge of the group. Now Pinky knew that Mrs. Lovebody had once owned a dog called Jack. When Jack died Mrs. Lovebody was heart-broken. She had no family and Jack had meant everything to her. Mrs. Lovebody had once worked for the vet in the neighbouring town so there wasn't much Mrs. Lovebody didn't know about dogs ! Now Pinky knew that Mrs. Lovebody said SHE WOULD NEVER HAVE ANOTHER

DOG but Pinky decided she would take a chance and pretending she hadn't noticed Mrs. Lovebody she said,

'What a pity this dog is in such a state ! There's only one person that I know who could save this dog and that's Mrs. Lovebody. There's not much she doesn't know about dogs is there? What a shame she doesn't want to own any more dogs !'

Everybody stood looking at the dog, nodding their heads in agreement. Suddenly, someone spoke out.

'I can do it. I can nurse this dog back to health. I know I can. Let me take him P.C. Probyn,' and saying this Mrs. Lovebody stooped over the dog to pick him up when P.C. Probyn replied.

' Well, I'm not sure about that Mrs. Lovebody. I think this dog's been through enough. What does everyone else think?'

'Well, I say let Mrs. Lovebody give it a go !' said Mrs. Sproggins in a brisk tone. 'And, I'm the head of this committee. Does anyone disagree with me?'

Now Mrs. Sproggins was very bossy and nobody wanted to upset her.

'Let's put it to the vote !' suggested P.C.

Probyn. 'All in favour of letting Mrs. Lovebody take the dog put one hand in the air. When everyone put a hand up in the air, he smiled and said, 'Well, there's no disagreement is there? Very well take the dog Mrs. Lovebody. But, I will be round to see you in a month's time and if he is no better I'm taking him back. Agreed?'

Mrs. Lovebody laughed and said 'One month ! The dog show is in one month. Not only will I nurse this dog back to health, he is going to be entered for the dog show. Whether he will have the waggiest tail or be the most handsome dog I can't say as yet. But, you wait and see, he is going to win something ! You mark my words !'

Everyone shook their heads in disbelief. Nursing the dog back to health was one thing. But, winning a prize? NEVER ! As it was now lunchtime, too polite to disagree with Mrs. Lovebody, everybody wished her luck with the dog and then went home.

Pinky walked part of the way home with Mrs. Lovebody who was carrying the dog in her arms as it was too weak from hunger to walk.

' Do you really think that you can save him?' enquired Pinky. 'Even his nose is dry and dirty when it should be wet and shiny. He's in a bad way isn't he?'

'He is poor chap, he is. Just have some faith Pinky. You'll see a different dog soon, believe me.' replied Mrs. Lovebody as she turned into the lane where she lived.

Pinky walked straight on, then Mrs. Lovebody called out,' you come and have a cuppa and a chat with me in a month's time and see if you don't see a difference in him. You just wait and see !'

Pinky walked home smiling to herself. She had pretended that she had doubts, but she had no doubts at all that Mrs. Lovebody could save the dog because Mrs. Lovebody had a huge heart and like her name she loved everybody !

As soon as she got home, Mrs. Lovebody gave a small amount of dog food to the dog who wolfed it down and looked for more. But Mrs. Lovebody knew that you had to take things slowly. The dog must eat small amounts of food for a time so not to upset his tummy. But she did fill up a big bowl of water and the dog drank every drop.

Now he had some company and was with someone that seemed to care about him, the dog perked up. As Mrs. Lovebody went around her cottage doing her chores the dog followed her everywhere. He even sat outside the toilet and waited for Mrs. Lovebody to come out ! He was very weak and tottered around. Sometimes he fell over but he picked himself up, determined to follow Mrs. Lovebody again. He didn't want to let her out of his sight !

'Right !' said Mrs. Lovebody to the dog. 'I'm going to give you a nice bath, then dry you and give your coat a brush. When I can see what sort of dog is under all that dirt, I can think about giving you a name.'

The dog began to wag his tail. Not that he knew what a bath was, but Mrs. Lovebody had a gentle voice so he thought in his doggy way that it must be something nice !

Surprisingly, although the dog had never had a bath before he found that he enjoyed it. The bath water was nice and warm and Mrs. Lovebody soaped him all over with her gentle hands and then poured some clean water over him to wash the soap suds away. She towelled him dry and switched on a hair dryer on a low heat so as not to scare him. Then, she began to brush the dog with a soft brush. The dog thought the treatment was lovely ! It was so good to feel clean again that he could not stop barking. 'Woof, woof, woofer ! Woof, woof, woofer !' On and on he barked, at the same time wagging his tail.

'Well !' remarked Mrs. Lovebody. 'It looks like you have chosen your own name, Woofer. Woofer it shall be then and you look so much better already. Well we will go for our walks at night when you are better. Nobody will be able to see how you are getting on. Then, I shall surprise them when I enter you for the dog show because goodness me, I think you are going to be a handsome dog when you put on some weight. You've got a lovely face haven't you? ' And with that she kissed him on his nose.

'Woof, woof, woofer !' replied Woofer. 'Woof, woof, woofer !' He felt like a different dog. A very hungry dog but goodness me ! Was that some more dog food Mrs. Lovebody was putting into his bowl ?

Mrs, Lovebody took Woofer to the vet the very next day to have him checked over.

'Well !' remarked the vet. 'He is in a bad way but he hasn't picked up any dog diseases. I will give him a vaccination against dog diseases so that he doesn't get any. He will have to have another injection soon so you need to make an appointment with the receptionist for that. I will give you some vitamin drops for him and some powders for his coat in case he has picked up any fleas. I think he is quite a young dog. Look at his teeth. They are nice and white and in good shape. I'd say he is probably around one year old so he will get bigger. Well, take good care of him Mrs. Lovebody and I will see you again soon. Good Luck !'

True to her word, nobody saw Mrs. Lovebody and Woofer for a month. Every evening when it got dark she took him for a long walk along the river bank. Woofer loved his walks ! There were so many lovely smells that other animals left around. Woofer smelled them all and wagged his tail a lot. He was a very happy dog. He had a good home, plenty to eat and a loving owner. What more could a dog want?

The dog show was on the last Saturday of that month. The village green was partly cordoned off and the villagers had brought chairs and blankets to sit on outside a large ring where the dog show would take place.

The first event was for the Dog With the Waggiest Tail. Twenty dogs were entered for this category. The smallest dog was a Jack Russell who wagged his tail so fast it almost made you cross-eyed watching it. Some dogs wagged their tails in slow loopy movements while other dogs just wagged their tails as fast as they could.

Mrs. Sproggins and Pinky sat at a table in the middle of the ring. The dog owners lined up with their dogs and waited for the result. After a lot of discussion with Pinky, Mrs. Sproggins walked over to the owner of the little Jack Russell and gave him a little silver cup. His dog had got the waggiest tail !

The next competition was to find the dog who could do the best tricks. There were dogs who could beg, lay down, roll over and walk on their hind legs. The dog who won the prize was a lovely collie dog who could dance to music, walk backwards on his hind legs and weave in and out of his owner's legs as he walked.

A pretty cocker spaniel won the prize for The Prettiest Dog and Pinky said to Mrs. Sproggins,

'Gosh ! Doesn't she remind you of Lady in the film 'Lady and the Tramp?'

'She certainly does look a bit like her,' agreed Mrs. Sproggins. 'But I think this little cocker spaniel Fudge is even prettier.'

Pinky nodded her head in agreement and then it was time for the last competition, to find the handsomest dog in the village. All the competitors lined up and just when Mrs. Sproggins and Pinky were about to walk along the line of owners with their dogs, someone shouted out,

'Wait for me ! I'm a bit late but I did send in my entry form in time.' Then, Mrs. Lovebody appeared with Woofer and joined the line of competitors.

'Oh !' gasped Pinky. 'Just look at Mrs. Lovebody's dog ! Why, he's just a, a, a....'

'Corker !' announced Mrs. Sproggins. ' He's an absolute corker. Just look at his coat !'

Woofer stood at the end of the line of dogs and their owners with Mrs. Lovebody. His fur was long, black and shone like silk. He had the most handsome face with large brown eyes and very long eyelashes. His ears were long and silky as was his plumed tail. It was anyone's guess what breed he was but who cared ? Woofer was without doubt THE MOST HANDSOME DOG IN THE VILLAGE AND HE DEFINITELY DESERVED THE PRIZE !!

Footy Freddy

Chapter Five

Every other Sunday morning there was a football match on the village green. The football team that represented the village Pinky lived in was called the Robindale Rovers. This Sunday, they were playing the Leofrick Lions. Nearly all the villagers turned up to support their team including Pinky. The football manager relied on Pinky to bring the fresh oranges for half time and give out the orange slices to the players. Pinky felt this was an honour because she had not been living in the village for very long.

The first half of the game looked promising for the Rovers. They scored a goal almost immediately but the Lions equalised and then scored another goal. Pinky knew most of the players but she liked to watch the star of their team Freddy, their centre forward. He was an amazing player ! He was brilliant at dribbling the ball, running rings around his opponents and then kicking or heading the ball into the net.

Suddenly, the Lions were in control of the ball and it looked like they might get the chance to score another goal. 'Oh, no ! Don't let them get another goal !' groaned Pinky as they sped down the field, efficiently passing the ball to one another. But then, Freddy held on to the player who had the ball by the arm and he couldn't free himself to give the ball a good kick. Pinky looked over at the referee but he hadn't seen Freddy do this. But Pinky had seen what Freddy had done and she didn't like it. Oh no, she didn't like it one little bit ! She wanted the Rovers to win but not by cheating !

Freddy had now got possession of the ball and wow ! He scored another goal ! The whole village cheered. 'Good on you Freddy !'someone shouted and Freddy raised his arms in the air and shouted in return, 'Ooh ah, Rovers are the best, I say the Rovers are the best !'

By half time Freddy had purposely tripped up three of the Lions' players when it looked like they might score a goal and deliberately held a player by his shirt. The referee didn't see any of Freddy's actions but Pinky did and it made her very angry.

.'Freddy is going to get our team a bad name !' she said crossly. 'I can't go and tell the referee to watch more carefully because he might think I'm accusing him of not doing his job properly.' But then, she had one of her FANTASTIC ideas.

Pinky handed a piece of sliced orange to each player at half time and then went to collect the pieces of orange peel afterwards. When she got to Freddy she looked down at his boots and pointing at them she said,

'Oh look at your football boots Freddy. They are so caked up with mud. We have still got a bit of time so why don't you give them to me and I'll scrape most of the mud off for you. The boots of the other players are nowhere near as muddy as yours, probably because you are the most active player we have got.'

'Oh okay. Ta very much !' Freddy replied. 'But don't take too long. We will be back in play again in a few minutes.' Pinky took the boots to her bag. She scraped off the worst of the mud and then got out some dubbin which she intended to put on the boots with a cloth. Now, Pinky always carried a few of her magic powders and potions with her because she never knew when they might be needed ! She mixed some magic powder into the dubbin and gave Freddy's boots a quick wipe over with the mixture.

Freddy was laughing and joking with some of the other players who were patting Freddy on the back. Pinky could hear them telling Freddy what a good player he was and that they couldn't do without him. 'Well, we could do without his cheating !' Pinky muttered to herself. 'Freddy is a brilliant player which is why it is so strange that he thinks it is all right to cheat !'

The referee blew his whistle and the game started again. The Rovers' goalie kicked the ball a long way down the pitch and Freddy got control of the ball at once. Then a most peculiar thing happened ! Freddy went to kick the ball to another player but his leg and foot moved in slow motion which allowed a player for the Lions to gain control of the ball. This happened several times. People began to shout at Freddy. 'Come on, Freddy ! What's the matter with you? We will lose the game at this rate!' But Freddy felt as though his feet and legs were weighed down by an iron ball and chain !

Finally, The Rovers' manager took Freddy out of the game and put Liam in instead. Liam was new to the village. He was just as good a player as Freddy but he had not yet been given the chance to prove it. Liam scored three goals for the Rovers who won the game by 5 to 2 goals.

'Hooray !' shouted Pinky with the other villagers. 'Well done the Rovers !'

Meanwhile the Rovers manager was having a

quiet word with Freddy.

'I just don't understand why you couldn't kick the ball properly in the second half. You were as slow as a snail and almost lost us the game. Well! I am sorry Freddy but I am pulling you out of the team for the next few games and putting Liam in instead. He's a great little player. Really! I just need players I can rely on and trust.'

Freddy bit his lip and looked miserable. He couldn't understand why he hadn't felt in control of his legs and feet. He went over to where Pinky was looking after the boys' bags and said to her,

'I can't believe it. I am being dropped from the team and goodness knows when I will be able to play again. Especially now that Liam has proved himself to be such a good player.'

'Yes.' replied Pinky. 'AND Liam doesn't trip up other players or hang on to their arms or shirts just to prevent them kicking the ball either.'

Freddy opened his mouth to protest but looking at Pinky's cross face he shut his mouth quickly. Pinky had obviously seen him and probably other people too. Because the referee had not seen him he thought he had got away with it. Suddenly, he felt ashamed !

Freddy didn't play for the team for a couple of months. When he was finally put back into play he made sure he didn't cheat again. It wasn't long before he regained his reputation as one of the Rovers' best players. Pinky's magic had taught him a valuable lesson, THAT IT'S JUST NOT WORTH CHEATING !

Poor Old Bessie

Chapter Six

Bessie, Farmer Brown's horse looked over the gate and watched the people who passed by. Some people cycled past, occasionally someone might walk past the field she was in and give her a pat on the nose but mostly people just hurried by without a glance in her direction.

Poor old Bessie was lonely. Farmer Brown was using his new tractor more and more and he decided he didn't need Bessie for farm work anymore. Bessie wished she had a companion; even a goat or donkey would do, but she heard Farmer Brown say he did not want any more animals on the farm other than his cows and chickens because they cost too much to feed.

Bessie was a big horse. Her colour was what people called dapple grey.
She had a kind eye and loved nothing more than a cuddle around her neck when she would lovingly nudge the person back with a soft neigh.

One day at the Saturday market, Pinky met Farmer Brown who had set up a stall to sell his eggs and butter.

'Hello Jim,' said Pinky to Farmer Brown. 'I see

you don't use Bessie very much now. She is in her field most days. Why is that?'

'Well !' remarked Farmer Brown. 'I don't really need her anymore. My tractor is much quicker and I have an open top lorry to stack hay, straw and other goods in. I was thinking that I would have to send her to the knacker's yard to be put down,'

'Why would you do that Jim? She isn't that old is she?' asked Pinky, looking concerned.

'I am afraid she is too old to sell. In the winter, I have to use a lot of straw for her stable and she eats so much hay because she is a big horse. No ! I have made my decision. I don't want to send her to the knacker's yard but she costs too much to keep. It's different with the cows and chickens because I make money from the sale of the milk, butter and eggs.'

'Oh dear !' replied Pinky sadly. 'I am so sorry to hear that because Bessie is such a kind horse and has served you well for years.'

'Yes, I know !' said Farmer Brown, shaking his head in sorrow. 'It doesn't seem fair but I am struggling to make my farm pay. People's eating habits have changed. They don't want my cabbages much anymore to go with a nice meat pie. They prefer chicken chow mein, chicken tikka or chicken korma. I am even thinking of cutting back the number of cauliflowers that I grow. They don't sell very well either. Excuse me now Pinky, I have a customer to serve,' and with that Farmer Brown turned away from Pinky who stood there, deep in thought and looking very sad, very sad indeed !

'Poor old Bessie !' she said out loud. 'I just have to do something to save her but what? Magic is not going to solve this problem is it?'

Pinky went home and made herself some tea in her favourite teapot with the pink roses on it. Then, she helped herself to two sticky buns. She sat down in a nice comfy armchair and thought about what could be done to save Bessie. After she had drunk three cups of tea, she felt all her parts had been refreshed and had a FANTABULOUS idea about how Bessie could pay for her upkeep. When she had stayed with her friend Izzy at the seaside, the donkey rides had been very popular. In fact, the donkeys were kept busy every day giving children rides up and down the beach. Why couldn't Farmer Brown use Bessie like that?

Pinky was so pleased with her idea that she hurried back to the market where Farmer Brown was just packing up the remains of his produce.

Not that there was much left because his chickens laid lovely, large, brown eggs and the butter he sold was delicious !

'Jim !' said Pinky, trying to attract his attention. 'I have a really good idea how Bessie could pay her way.'

'Really ?' replied Jim Brown. 'Well, I have tried to solve the problem. I even thought I could rent Bessie out to be used but there are some horrible people in this world. I wouldn't want to see her overworked at her age. So, go on Pinky. What's your idea then?'

'Well !' said Pinky excitedly. 'Couldn't you put an advert in the local paper to say Bessie will give rides to children around one of your fields. I'm sure people would pay a good price. Also,' she added, enthusiastically. 'Mrs. Brown could sell cups of tea and coffee with some of her delicious scones with cream and jam to the parents while they wait for their children's rides to finish.'

'Goodness me !' exclaimed Jim Brown. 'Now, why didn't I think of that. That really is a topping idea Pinky. My wife would love to sell some of her home-made cakes too, especially if it means we can keep poor old Bessie after all.'

'Yes,' laughed Pinky. 'But you have to promise

me something in return.'

'Oh really. What's that then ?' asked Farmer Brown, looking puzzled and taking off his cap, he scratched his head.

'That I can be the first customer to have a ride on lovely old Bessie AND get a free cup of tea AND a free scone with cream and jam as well.'

'Done !' laughed Jim Brown. 'You strike a hard bargain Pinky !' Then, when he saw Pinky's downcast face, he added, 'I'm only joking ! You can have your horse ride and tea and scone because you have certainly earned it !'

True to his word, Farmer Brown phoned the local newspaper and placed an advert in the advertisement section and this is what it said;

> Come and ride Bessie the farm horse at Brown's Farm.
> Rides available after school on weekdays and Saturdays. £3 for a ride around the big field.
> Refreshments such as tea, coffee, home made cake and buttered scones will be on sale also.

Pinky read the advertisement and couldn't

wait for Saturday to come. She had never ridden a horse before but she wasn't worried because she could trust Bessie. She was such a kind, gentle horse !

When Saturday arrived, Pinky put on a pair of pink and white patterned zigzag trousers with a plain pink jumper. Then she put on a pair of brown, sturdy boots. Then leaving her cat Sydney some nice fish for his breakfast she set off for the farm to arrive at 9 o'clock.

'Goodness me !' exclaimed Pinky when she saw a long queue of children standing outside Bessie's field which was opposite the back of Farmer Brown's house. 'But at least I will be first to have a ride. Then, I can have my free tea and cake. I can still get back to open my shop at 10 o'clock.'

Pinky really enjoyed her ride on Bessie. Farmer Brown helped her to get on Bessie's broad back. She felt like a princess, Princess Pinky, as she walked and then trotted around the field. She waved to all the parents and children and they waved back. Pinky was well loved in the village because she was wise, kind, funny and everyone loved her lovely sweets !

When Pinky reached the gate and got off, the first child in the queue was helped onto Bessie.

The children were now chattering excitedly while their parents sat on chairs at tables which Mrs. Brown had set out on the patio.

Pinky went to sit at a small table but was soon called over to join some of her neighbours. She ordered a cup of tea and ate a whopping piece of delicious cake with strawberries on top while she told her friends how it had been her idea for Bessie to give rides to earn her keep.

Just then Mrs. Brown called Pinky over to where she was serving teas, coffees and cake.

'Thank you so much Pinky.' said Mrs. Brown. 'I think your idea is a great success ! Just look at how much money I have made already from the refreshments. She showed Pinky a pot stuffed full of bank notes and coins. 'There's enough there to pay for hay and straw for a while so we will be able to keep Bessie after all.'

' Yes I'm pleased too,' replied Pinky, beaming at Mrs. Brown. Then as she turned to walk along the outside of Bessie's field on her way home Bessie nickered and neighed to Pinky, a very loud horsey thank you !

Pinky and the Love Hearts

Chapter Seven

Pinky was busy in her shop making new displays of her sweets. All sweets were now grouped in their colours. So, it didn't matter whether they were licky ones, chewy ones or fizzy ones as long as they were the same colour they were in a section of their own. Just one section had a mix of coloured sweets because the sweets were candy striped, multi coloured or needed to be together. But the shop filled up with people and so Pinky would have to finish the displays later. Miss Blush was at the front of the queue followed by Mr. Hart.

'Hello ! Miss Blush. How are you these days?' asked Mr. Hart. But just like her name Miss Blush's cheeks went bright pink and she turned without answering and said to Pinky,

'I have to rush, I'll come back later.'

How odd, thought Pinky. She's only just arrived and now she's leaving again.

'What would you like Mr. Hart? Liquorice, toffee, chocolate?' Pinky enquired.

'Can I have some Happy Humbugs please Pinky? 'I need something to cheer me up,' he said looking at Miss Blush as she left the shop. Pinky weighed the sweets on the scales and then put them into a little bag which she twisted at the top to seal it.

When Mr. Hart had left the shop, the next customer Miss Driver was tut-tutting and shaking her head as she chattered to another customer Mrs. Powney.

'I just don't understand those two !' Miss Driver said. 'Everyone in the village knows they are madly in love with one another. In fact, ever since they were at school together.'

'Yes,' agreed Mrs. Powney. 'But Connor Hart is too shy to ask Ariadne Blush to go out with him. And, Ariadne won't even look at Connor because she worries he might see that she likes him.'

' Well, it's been years since they left school and they are no nearer settling down with one another and I don't think they ever will.' said Miss Driver, shaking her head.

'Well, Ariadne lives at one end of the village and Connor lives at the other end so they hardly ever meet up. Such a shame !' remarked another customer.

Everyone in the shop began to chat about the lack of friendship between Ariadne Blush and

Connor Hart. They all agreed that it was such a pity that the couple were both too shy to admit they liked one another.

When Pinky had served the last customer she turned the shop sign on the door from 'open' to 'closed' and then had a quick lunch. She needed to finish the sweet displays and then as she glanced at the sweets which were called love hearts, she had a WONDERFUL idea ! Something must be done to get Ariadne and Connor together and she was just the person to do it ! The love hearts were in different colours and had different little messages on them such as 'you are handsome',' you have a lovely smile',' pretty girl,' 'kiss me', 'I love you,' and 'please marry me.' Well, thought Pinky. If they are too shy to talk to one another the love hearts could talk for them ! Yes ! I think I could work something out with these sweets. Pinky thought she had the most amazing ideas and she did !

The next time Miss Blush came into the shop she asked Pinky for a box of Crackle Candies.

'Oh thank you Pinky !' said Ariadne. 'I was thinking of going to the cinema soon and I wanted to take some of your sweets with me.' Just as she was leaving the shop Pinky called her back.

'Connor Hart has left a little package for you Ariadne,' said Pinky.

'Really?' commented Ariadne. She did look pleased. 'I wonder what it can be?'

Pinky handed over the package to Ariadne. 'There you are. Are you going to open it now?' Pinky asked.

'No, I'll open it later.' Ariadne began to blush just thinking about Connor. But as soon as she got outside the shop she couldn't wait to open the package. In it were two lovely little love hearts. One said, 'you have a lovely smile,' the other one said ,'pretty girl.'

Why, Connor thinks I am pretty and I have a lovely smile. Perhaps he likes me a little bit after all ! thought Ariadne. She felt exceedingly happy. She got the next bus into town to do some shopping and to see which films were showing at the cinema.

Pinky thought it was a big coincidence that Connor Hart came into her shop just an hour later.

'Have you got any of your Whizzing Whoppers?' asked Connor. 'I am thinking of going to the cinema soon and I love your Whizzing Whoppers. They last for ages, so you don't need to eat more than a few at a time. I have to watch my weight you know,' he said laughing. 'Otherwise I'll never get a girlfriend !'

Pinky smiled at him and thought to herself, I think you are going to get a girlfriend sooner than you think and one that you have always wanted too. But, I'm not going to spoil the surprise and tell you that !

'Oh by the way Connor.' Pinky said. 'I've got a little package that Ariadne Blush left for you. I think you had better take it now.' Pinky handed over a little package with Connor's name on it.

'I am surprised ! What can it be?' Connor opened the package and took out a little love heart which said, 'you are handsome.'

'Wow ! Just look at this Pinky.' said Connor smiling happily. 'And there was me thinking that Ariadne has never noticed me. Well, I never. This has made my day.'

Connor went out and whistling cheerfully he went home to look in the local newspaper to see what films were showing at the cinema in town.

Pinky was very pleased with herself. She wasn't going to tell anyone about the love heart messages on the sweets she was packaging up and giving to Ariadne and Connor. It was a step in the right direction. Yes, it was !

It was two days before Saturday when Ariadne Blush came into Pinky's shop again and she ACTUALLY asked Pinky if there were any more little packages for her.

'Oh, yes !' said Pinky. 'Connor left a bigger package for you this time. Ariadne took the package and opened it immediately. Three little love hearts fell out. The first said 'be mine,' the second said 'kiss me,' and the third one said 'I love you.'

'Oh !' gasped Ariadne. 'Connor does care for me after all and there was I thinking he wasn't interested in me. These little love hearts have made me so happy. I am so, so happy.' She began to twirl and dance around the shop then coming to a standstill she said,' I think I need to buy some love hearts for Connor. Will you help me pick some out, Pinky?'

Together, the two friends sorted through the love hearts with some tongs.

'What about this one?' asked Pinky. 'Look, it says, 'I love you too.'

'Oh yes. That's a good one isn't it? Do you know Pinky I was in the same class as Connor at school and I loved him from the first time I saw him but I never dared to tell him how I felt.'

'Well !' Pinky replied. 'He obviously loves you

too otherwise he wouldn't have bothered to leave these little packages for you would he?'

Pinky and Ariadne continued to sort through the rest of the love hearts. 'What about this one?' suggested Pinky triumphantly holding up a big love heart.

'What does it say? What does it say?' said Ariadne snatching the love heart from Pinky. 'Oh look !' It says, 'take me out.' I say, it's not too daring is it Pinky? I've known Connor for a long time but I don't want to overdo it, do I?' Ariadne said blushing to the roots of her hair.

'No !' I don't think it is too daring,' said Pinky firmly. 'I think Connor would like to take you out but he's too shy to ask you. But now this little love heart is doing the asking for both of you instead.'

Ariadne asked Pinky to wrap up the two love hearts and Ariadne wrote Connor's name on it. She gave it to Pinky and said,' will you give this to Connor and tell him I will be waiting outside the cinema in town at 11.00 o'clock Saturday morning. It's up to him now isn't it?'

On Friday morning Connor came to Pinky's shop for some more sweets.

'I need some sweets to take to the cinema' he said. 'There is a really good film on tomorrow.' Then, shyly he asked,' I suppose it's too much to ask if there are any more packages for me?'

'Oh yes indeed !' Here you are.' replied Pinky as she handed over Ariadne's little package. 'Ariadne wants you to meet her at the cinema at 11.00 o'clock tomorrow morning.'

' Really?' said Connor as he opened the package carefully and looking at the love hearts he said. 'I can't believe it. Look Pinky ! Ariadne has given me a love heart which says she loves me. Well ! Ariadne and I have wasted too much time already. Can you find me a love heart which says 'will you marry me' and put it into a special box. I will certainly meet her at the cinema. I can't wait for tomorrow to come AND I am going to give her the box with the 'marry me' love heart and hope for the best. Do wish me luck ! '

Pinky put the love heart in a little box decorated with red hearts. As she handed it to Connor she said,' you won't need any luck Connor. It's clear you two are made for one another but you just didn't know it.'

Connor and Ariadne really enjoyed the film at the cinema and three months later an announcement appeared in the local paper which said;

> Miss Ariadne Blush and Mr. Connor Hart will be married at 2.00 o'clock on Saturday, 5th September at St. David's Church. Everyone in the village will be welcome to attend
> the wedding and many of you by invitation will be requested to help the happy couple celebrate afterwards as there
> will be a buffet and dancing in the village hall.

Pinky read the notice and went upstairs immediately to choose an outfit to wear for the wedding. She chose a pink dress with golden stars printed on it, pink satin shoes and a saucy, little, pink hat adorned with a gold heart on one side. Too much pink? Pinky didn't think so ! She couldn't wait to go to the wedding. AND SHE DESERVED THE WEDDING INVITATION THAT ARRIVED IN THE POST THE NEXT DAY DIDN'T SHE? YES, SHE DID !

Chimpy and Chee Chee

Chapter Eight

One morning, Pinky got out of bed and looked out of her window. She was delighted to see a circus had arrived in the village and already caravans were parked on the village green. Some of the circus people were putting up the Big Top where all the circus acts would take place. Some of the caravans showed pictures of the performers in the circus. There would be acrobats, trapeze artists, bareback horse riders, three clowns Stinky, Binky and Bobbo and a chimpanzees' tea party to name a few of the acts.

'Wow !' said Pinky out loud. 'How exciting ! I haven't been to a circus since I was a little girl. A visit to the circus would be amazing.' Pinky opened her shop right on the dot of 9.00 o'clock and straight away the shop was full of people chatting about the circus.

'Has this circus been here before?' Pinky asked her first customer, Mrs. Gavin.

'Oh yes. It arrives here every year but we never know which week it will come here.'

'Yes.' added Mrs Hatch. 'That's a nuisance

really because if you are away on holiday it means you would miss seeing it which is such a shame !'

'Well, when will we be able to buy the tickets to see the show?' Pinky asked.

'Oh, don't you worry about that,' chorused two of her customers. 'The tickets will be available by teatime today. There will be a booth selling the tickets by the play area. That's where the circus people usually put it.'

'Oh goody !' exclaimed Pinky. 'I'll make sure that I go to the booth early. I do want a front row ticket and they might sell out quickly.'

Pinky finished serving her customers and then thought that she would go over and see how the circus people were getting on with setting things up.

One of the clowns came out of a caravan. Pinky could see it was Stinky the clown because he had a big hat with his name on the front of it. In fact, he had all his clown clothes on. He wore a blue and white striped play suit with big, white bobbles down the front of it and very large flapping shoes that went flip, flap, plink, plonk on the ground.

'Hello !' said Pinky. 'Can you tell me when the circus will be open and how much the tickets are please?'

Stinky grinned at Pinky and said,

'The circus will start
With raspberry tart.
At exactly four,
Don't ask me more.
Front row will be
In pounds, two and three.
The rest of the benches
Each cost five fifty pences.'
Now riddlely- me- ree,
It's time for my tea !

Then Stinky turned around and flip, flap, plink, plonk he flapped his way back to his caravan.

'What a funny man !' giggled Pinky. 'Well, I suppose that's because he's a clown. I wonder if he talks in riddles all the time. I guess I will have to wait until I go to the show to find that out.' Saying this, Pinky went back to her shop but by 5 o'clock she could see that the ticket booth was open.

She went to get her purse and took out the exact amount of money needed for a front row ticket, £5. She was about to go to her friend Queenie's house to see if Queenie wanted to go to the circus when she remembered Queenie was away on holiday. Pinky bought a front row ticket for the end of the week on Saturday.

The week seemed to go slowly, but finally Saturday arrived and Pinky kept herself busy all day to keep her mind off the circus. She was so excited and couldn't wait to go ! Finally, it was time and Pinky shut the shop and arrived just before four o'clock. The Big Top was filling up quickly. Most of the people from the village were there as well as people from other villages.

Pinky thought the show was amazing ! There were three trapeze artists and acrobats who walked on high wires. So daring ! Pinky thought. The bareback horse riders were two teenagers, a boy and girl who could run along the sides of the horses, jump onto one and then jump onto another horse without losing their balance. Binky and Bobbo the clowns were fired from an enormous cannon to land safely in a net on the other side of the circus. It was all so exciting but it was the chimpanzees' tea party that stole the show !

Chimpy and Chee Chee came into the circus ring holding hands. Chimpy wore red shorts and a white shirt with a red bow tie. Chee Chee wore a red and white spotted dress with an alice band decorated with red flowers on her head. Chimpy went to fetch a shopping trolley then he and Chee Chee went to a little shop that was set up for them. Chattering to one another, they pointed to the items they wanted to buy and Chee Chee took out a purse from her little red handbag and paid the shopkeeper.

The two chimps pushed the trolley to a small house and put all the shopping things in a cupboard. All except the things they wanted for their tea party of course ! Chimpy put a table cloth on a little table and Chee Chee laid the table with a teapot, sugar bowl, milk jug, cups, saucers and some plates. Then, Chimpy went to the cupboard and fetched a chocolate cake. Chee Chee cut two big slices of cake and poured out the tea into the cups. How polite they were to start with ! Although Chimpy did pour his tea into a saucer and slurped the tea from the saucer while Chee Chee drank her tea daintily from a cup.

Soon, Chimpy decided he didn't like the cake and started to throw it at Chee Chee who chased Chimpy around the circus ring, trying to pour the rest of the tea in the teapot over him. Finally, they threw the teapot and remains of the cake away and cuddled one another instead.

As soon as they scurried out of the ring the audience stood up calling 'Encore ! Encore !' to get the chimps back again.

The chimps did come back but this time they were riding bicycles and squirted water from water pistols over the people sitting in the front rows as they rode around the ring. Finally, the show came to an end after the clowns had a pie fight and threw pails of water over one another.

Pinky went home after the show which she thought was thrilling. In fact, she enjoyed it so much that she decided to see the Sunday show as well. It would be the last show and the circus would move on somewhere else on the Monday.

'Yes,' she said aloud. 'I will go and see the show just one more time because I did enjoy the chimpanzees' tea party so much.' She thought the show was definitely worth the money. But sadly, on Sunday, the chimpanzees did not appear in the show. You must be wondering why that was ! Well, during the night something very bad happened to Chimpy and Chee Chee.

Chimpy and Chee Chee slept in their own little caravan which had been made especially for them. Inside the caravan was a small table and chairs, two armchairs, a cupboard and two bunk beds. Chimpy slept on the bottom bunk and Chee Chee on the top bunk.

At about one o'clock in the morning a mean, nasty man and lady opened the caravan door and climbing into the caravan they picked the little chimpanzees up and put them in a wire cage. Chimpy woke up and began to scream and chatter loudly. At once, the lady injected Chimpy with a drug to make him sleepy. Just in case Chee Chee woke up the lady injected her with the drug as well. All the circus people were asleep in their caravans and sadly nobody heard anything.

In the morning, the two chimpanzees woke up to find themselves in a big room. There were animals of all kinds in different size cages. There was a beautiful Persian cat with green eyes, two parrots, three dogs and some chinchilla rabbits. Lastly, there was a big snake curled up in a glass container.

Suddenly, the door opened and the man and lady came into the room. The lady put down a bunch of keys close to the chimpanzees' cage and then walked to the other end of the room where the snake was. The lady called to the man, and together the couple peered at the snake and talked in low whispers to one another. While their backs were turned, Chimpy put his hand through the cage he was in and picked up the bunch of keys. He sat on them quickly and put his finger to his lips so that Chee Chee didn't make a sound. Chimpy was not only clever, he was a quick thinker too !

'Well !' said the man. 'We have got a rich buyer for this lot. He has a big collection of stuffed animals already but needs a few more for his display. He will pick the best of these creatures and sell on the ones he doesn't want. Who to? I don't care as long as he pays us good money for them !'

Chimpy and Chee Chee didn't know what the man meant by stuffed animals but they didn't like the sound of the man's menacing voice. No, they didn't !

'Oh !' exclaimed the lady. 'I thought I put my keys down on this table top but they are not there. Perhaps I left them in the office. Well, let's go and have some lunch in the restaurant next door. Then, I will look for the keys so we can unlock the lorry doors and load all of these cages in the back.'

'Yeah ! Good idea. Let's go. We have got plenty of time. The buyer doesn't want these animals delivered until lunch time. Then, we will have the money to book that holiday we want,' the man replied.

As the couple left the room, the man took a key from his pocket and locked the door of the room the animals were in. None of the animals liked being in the cages. They were hungry, thirsty and just wanted to go home.

Chimpy now got up and picked up the lady's keys he had been sitting on. He tried each key in the cage they were in and suddenly, click, the door sprang open and the two chimpanzees climbed out. Chimpy went to each of the cages and unlocked the doors. As the snake was in a big glass container Chimpy kept hitting one side with the keys until it cracked. Then, Chimpy struck the glass one more time and it smashed. Now they were all free but there still remained one problem. How were they to get out of the room?

All the animals were connected by one thought, how could they escape? Well, the snake led the way. He slithered over to the window which was open. He hooked his head into a tie back on the curtains and let his body slither down the outside wall. The snake had made his body into a long rope !

Chimpy was the first to hold the snake's body

and let himself down to the ground followed by Chee Chee. The other animals followed, gripping the snake tightly, they too climbed down the snake's body. The parrots simply flew away, their brightly coloured feathers gleaming in the sun shine. Lastly, the snake unhooked his head and slithered down the wall. They were all free and they scattered in all directions !

Chimpy and Chee Chee looked around them. They were in one of three connecting alleys that led to the high street of the town. They scampered to the top of one of the alleys and looked up and down the street. Now, Chimpy could not read but he recognised the letters on a van parked outside a baker's shop. He had seen that van parked outside the bakery in the village where the circus was. The letters on the van spelled out Bert Bentham's Bakery.

Taking Chee Chee's hand, Chimpy pointed to the van and chattered to Chee Chee who understood at once what Chimpy wanted them to do. Both chimps scampered across the road. (yes, they did look both ways first to make sure there were no cars or buses coming) Opening one of the back doors, they climbed in and snuggled down behind a packing case. They didn't make a sound !

It wasn't long before Mr. Bentham came out of the town's bakery and climbing into his van, he set off for home. Once he was back in the village, Mr. Bentham went into his house to have his dinner. The chimpanzees waited for a few minutes and then quietly clambered out of the van. They looked around them. Where was the circus, the Big Top and the circus people? Sadly, it was now Monday and the circus had packed up and moved on to the next town !

Jerry Jolley who owned the chimpanzees had put up posters all around the village which gave his phone number should the chimps be found. He would then come back to collect them. Jerry loved his little chimps and the two little chimps loved Jerry. Jerry had rescued the chimps when they were babies. They had been stolen from their mother by a poacher in a far away country in Africa. Jerry was on holiday there and bought the chimps to save them from their miserable lives.

Jerry had not wanted to give the chimps to a zoo. Instead, he had made them their own little caravan and taught them to perform in the circus ring. Chimpy and Chee Chee loved to show off to the audiences and were adored by all the circus folk. They had all the freedom they wanted. They would play with the circus children and of course as brother and sister they had one another to love.

Once, Jerry had showed the two chimps a picture of a jungle where lots of chimps were climbing and swinging from trees. Jerry wanted them to know where they had come from. Now, seeing that the circus had gone, Chimpy looked over to the edge of the woods. There are a lot of trees over there, he said to himself. It must be a jungle !

It was at that moment that Pinky looked across the village green and saw the chimps standing outside the baker's shop. She had no idea how the chimps had suddenly appeared but she didn't want to frighten them. Before she could do anything, Chimpy and Chee Chee set off for the woods and disappeared from sight !

Pinky followed the chimps and going into the woods she called out their names, 'Chimpy, Chee Chee where are you?' Looking up, Pinky suddenly saw two little, hairy faces peeping through the branches of a tree. But the chimps didn't know Pinky, she wasn't their beloved Jerry so they wouldn't climb down. They preferred the safety of the trees !

Pinky went back home and telephoned Jerry

but he wasn't able to travel to the village straight away. Pinky didn't want the chimps to go any further into the woods in case they got lost and might be difficult to find. Just then Pinky had a FANTASTICAL idea ! She took some sweets called Banana Beauties and put them into a box. These sweets tasted like bananas and looked like bananas. Perhaps she could tempt the chimps with the sweets for they must be very hungry by now she thought. Pinky telephoned Jerry again and told him that she had a good plan to get the chimps to come to her shop and would he collect them there when he could.

Pinky went back to the woods and finding that the two little chimps were still in the same tree she began to drop the Banana Beauties on the ground. She walked slowly back across the village green leaving a long line of Banana Beauties leading to her shop.

Chimpy and Chee Chee looked down from their tree and could see and smell what they thought were real bananas ! Chattering to one another they climbed down from the tree and began to eat the sweets.

'Mm, just gorgeous !' Chimpy said to Chee Chee in chimpy chat. Chee Chee didn't even look up ! She was too busy stuffing her mouth with the Banana Beauties ! It took a long time, but the two chimps followed the Banana Beauties trail, picking up a few of the sweets at a time, then sitting down again to enjoy eating them. Suddenly, Chee Chee looked over to Pinky's shop and saw her beloved Jerry standing outside. Clutching the rest of the sweets in their hands the chimps scampered over to Jerry and jumped into his loving arms. They began to pat Jerry's head and covered his face with slobbery kisses at the same time chatting in their chimp language. 'Ooh, ooh,' ooh, ooh !'

Pinky was so pleased that her plan had worked; that Jerry and the chimps were together once more, that she invited the three of them in for a cup of tea. Chee Chee took the big pink tea pot with the pink roses on it and poured out four cups of tea. Chimpy cut the cherry cake that Pinky put on the table. Both chimps began to slurp the tea from their cups and smacked their lips to show their appreciation of Pinky's cake.

'Well! Wherever they have been, they haven't forgotten how to pour out the tea and cut the cake, have they Pinky ?' said Jerry, a big smile on his face.

'No, and I don't think we will ever know what

happened to them. But, they are certainly happy to be back with you.' replied Pinky as she watched Chee Chee climb on to Jerry's lap for a cuddle. It wasn't long before Chimpy pushed Chee Chee off of Jerry's lap and climbed onto Jerry's lap instead. Then, the two chimps began to fight, rubbing the rest of their cake into one another's faces. Pinky and Jerry roared with laughter and pulling them apart they took one chimp each onto their laps.

Before Jerry took the chimps back to the circus he took the chimps back to the edge of the woods so that they could play amongst the trees. Chattering to Jerry as they swung from tree to tree, Chee Chee called out in chimpy chat. ' Look at me ! Look at me, Jerry !' Finally, Jerry called to them to come down from the trees and cuddling them in his arms he took them back to his car and drove back to the circus.

The circus folk were so pleased to see the chimps for everybody had missed them very much. Yes, it was a happy ending all because of Chimpy's clever actions and Pinky's Banana Beauties !!

Tibbs's Troubles

Chapter Nine

Besides her new range of sweets called FUN SWEETS, Pinky had also created a range of sweets called SURPRISE SWEETS. The surprise sweets had different textures to them. So, you might have to lick them to start with, then suck them, then chew them perhaps suck them again until you got to the centre and it was anyone's guess what could be in the middle ! What do you think could be in the middle?

One Sunday morning, Pinky got up early to make some surprise sweets but went to the front door to let Sidney, her cat out. To her surprise a little girl was sitting on the front step, crying.

'Goodness, gracious me !' exclaimed Pinky. 'The shop is not open today as it is Sunday.' she said. Then, peering closer at the little girl she asked. 'Are n't you Tanny Tibbs? You were the little girl who guessed the correct weight of my Extraordinary, Egnormous Easter Egg that had a magic wish in it weren't you?'

'Yes, yes Mrs. Spinks. And, I've come to ask you if you could give me another magic wish.

Could you? I need one badly.'

'What on earth for?' exclaimed Pinky. 'Magic wishes are very hard to make. I can't just dish them out like sweets. Why do you need one Tanny?'

'Well, Daddy has got a job as an odd job man with a travelling fairground and Mummy is ill in bed. She says she is up all night cos our baby Alfie is teething and crying through the night. Mummy says she is so tired, that our home is in a mess and that we are all becoming hooligans. There are eight of us children and I don't know when Daddy will be home to help,' she said, beginning to sob loudly.

'Oh dear, oh dear !' Pinky exclaimed. 'But these sorts of troubles can't be magicked away, they need to be sorted out. Well, I was just going to cook my breakfast but perhaps I should cook breakfast for all of your family instead.'

'Oh, would you Mrs. Spinks? I knew I should come to you for help even if you can't give me a magic wish.' Tanny said in a hopeful voice. 'Oh do come now, please do.'

So, Pinky packed a big pink and white striped bag with some eggs, bacon, sausages, mushrooms, tomatoes, two tins of baked beans and a large crusty loaf of bread, a packet of butter and a big jar of plum jam. She added a big box of Squidgy Squiggles as already she had an idea as to how she could help Tanny's family.

Together, Pinky and Tanny went across the village green and turned into a narrow lane. Pinky followed Tanny to the end of the lane where there were four cottages. In front of the last cottage there was a field where children of all ages were playing football.

'This is our cottage,' said Tanny. 'What do you think it is called ?'

'Well,' said Pinky. 'My guess is it is End Cottage. Am I right? It is the obvious choice for a name now isn't it?'

Just then, the children saw Pinky and Tanny and whooping with delight they ran over to where they were standing. Pinky noticed that they all looked untidy. They all had dirty shoes and trainers on and some of them had torn clothes and holes in their socks. The smallest girl said,

'Have you brought us some sweeties Mrs. Spinks? Oh, do say you have. Mummy and Daddy can't afford to buy us sweets very often.'

'Well,' replied Pinky, smiling at them all. 'You will soon find that out ! But, let's go into your cottage first because there is something I want to talk to you all about.'

Tanny led the way and Pinky followed her into a small but bright, sun shiny kitchen and sat herself down at the kitchen table. The children stood around her, wondering why Pinky had come to their cottage. Tanny introduced them all to Pinky, pointing to each child in turn.

'These two are Perdita and Prudence, we call them Perdy and Prue for short. They are twins and fourteen years old. Tyrone is the eldest but he works for Farmer Brown now so he will be here later.'

'Yes, I have met Tyrone once or twice.' Pinky said with a twinkle in her eye. For once, she had given Tyrone a magic Grinning Gobstopper when he had behaved badly in her shop !

'Well, the next eldest are Tommy and Sean. They are twins too. I am next as I am eleven years old. My name is Tanya but I am called Tanny for short. Then there is Pamela, we call her Plum, she's eight and lastly our baby brother Alfie is upstairs with Mummy.'

'Righty ho !' Pinky said. 'Well, you all know who I am and I've come here this morning to cook you all a lovely breakfast and one for your Mum too. Then, after breakfast, we are all going to sit down at the table and work out a plan to help your Mum. It must be a lot of work to look after you all, I am sure.' For looking around her, Pinky could see piles of unwashed clothes dumped on the kitchen floor, piles of unwashed dishes in the sink and the windows looked grimy.

'Firstly, I want two volunteers to wash and dry some plates we can use for our breakfast. Someone else can lay the table and the rest of you can tidy this room so we all have a seat to sit on.' Pinky began to get out all the food she was going to cook and put it next to the cooker.

When the children saw what Pinky was going to cook for breakfast they rushed around the kitchen doing what Pinky had asked them to do. Perdy and Prue cleared all the dirty clothes away then laid the table. Tommy and Sean went into the garden and picked some flowers. These made a colourful display in the middle of the table in an old vase they had found. Tanny cut up the whole loaf that Pinky had brought and Plum buttered the slices. The large pot of plum jam was given centre place next to the bread and butter. Finally, Prue made a big pot of tea. They sat at the table sniffing the lovely aroma of the eggs, sausages and bacon frying in two enormous pans on the top of the stove.

'Coo, doesn't it smell lovely !' said Sean. It

was a long time since they had such a big breakfast. Once Pinky had given each of them a big plate of cooked food she went upstairs with a tray laden with a lovely breakfast and a cup of tea for Mrs. Tibbs.

'Here you are Mrs. Tibbs.' Pinky said brightly. 'You just tuck into this lovely breakfast. You need to keep your strength up.' Then, going over to Alfie's cot she slipped a Sunny Soother into his mouth for he had been bawling loudly,' wa-ah, wa-ah !' At once Alfie stopped crying. 'Goo, goo, ga, ga,' he said. The Sunny Soother was made of honey. It quickly melted in his mouth soothing his sore gums where his two front teeth were coming through.

'Bless you Mrs. Spinks !' said Mrs. Tibbs as she sat up to eat the scrumptious breakfast. ' Oh and bless Alfie. Look, he's fallen asleep.' Alfie, who was twenty months old, was snoring in baby huffs and puffs. Laying on his back with his chubby arms stretched up above him, he looked like a little angel with his lovely rosy cheeks.

'Well !' commented Pinky. 'You wouldn't think Alfie could cry so loudly when you look at him now. You enjoy your breakfast Mrs. Tibbs and I will send one of the children up to collect the tray. If I were you I would have a little sleep while Alfie is sleeping.'

Pinky went back downstairs and joined the children at the table. When they had finished their breakfast, Pinky cleared away the dishes and told Tommy and Sean to fetch a big piece of paper and a pen.

'Look !' she said. 'I am going to draw a big grid on the paper with your names down the side. At the top of the paper I will write the days of the week. Now, you Perdy will wash and iron the family's clothes. You can do this after school. I should hang the wet clothes out on the clothes line on nice days and tumble dry them on wet days. When you have done this you must put a tick on the sheet on the right day to show that the job is done. Tommy and Sean you can do the shopping every day. Prue, you can cook the meals. Tanny told me that you won a prize at school for cookery so you are the best person for that job. Tanny and Plum, your job is to keep the house tidy. Make sure everybody puts their clothes and belongings away. Again, you all put a tick on the chart to show you have completed your jobs. Do you all agree?'

The children looked at one another and

nodded their heads. They could see that what Pinky said made sense. Sharing out the work meant Mrs. Tibbs would have more time to look after Alfie and have time to rest as well.

'Now !' Pinky laughed. 'I think these are what you have been waiting for,' AND she put the big box of Squidgy Squiggles on the table. Prue counted the sweets out and everybody got an equal share. There were cries of delight as they all tried the different flavoured sweets.

'They are so tasty,' grinned Sean as he pulled and stretched a Squidgy Squiggle out of his mouth. 'Mine is raspberry flavour and it's gorgeous,' he added.

'Cor ! Just look !' Tommy said as he stretched out his squiggles so that they spelled out his name in joined up writing. 'Don't they go a long way. I bet you could even write a story with them all if you stuck them on some paper. But, it would be a bit of a waste when they taste so nice.' He stuffed some into his mouth and beamed at everyone. 'Just scrumptious,' he said, grinning at everyone.

Pinky decided it was time for her to go. She needed to make some more sweets to sell in her shop. She had not used any magic to sort out the Tibbs family so that everything went smoothly. But she didn't mind, oh no she didn't ! For the next Sunday she saw the whole Tibbs family going to church. They all had their Sunday best clothes on and looked very nice. Pinky went over to them and said,

'Hello. You all look very nice. How is Alfie now?'

'Oh hello, Pinky. Thank you so much for organising my household until I got better. Also, Mr. Tibbs didn't like the job he took with the fairground and is back home and doing jobs in the village once again. And, just look at our Alfie!' Mrs. Tibbs beamed proudly. 'He's got his front teeth through at last !'

Pinky looked at Alfie and tickled his tummy. In return, Alfie beamed at her and said, 'goo, goo Pinky. Goo goo.'

'Goodness gracious !' gasped Mrs. Tibbs. 'He's just said his first word and it's your name Pinky. Well, I never !'

Pinky didn't see much of the Tibbs family after that. But, one day Mrs. Tibbs came into the shop to buy some sweets. There was two-year-old Alfie holding his mother's hand.

'I don't suppose you remember me, do you Alfie?' Pinky asked.

'Yes, me do !' he answered in a firm voice.

'And me want Widgy Widdles pease.'

'Don't you mean Squidgy Squiggles?' Pinky asked.

'Yes, me does,' answered Alfie, nodding his head. Then he gave Pinky a big smile which showed all of his new and pearly white teeth !!

The Fancy Dress Competition

Chapter Ten

It was the end of the school holidays but it was not the end of the fun events in the village where Pinky lived. Oh no ! There was a new mayor taking up office in the nearby town and it was decided that there would be fancy dress competitions to celebrate. The mayor would go to each village surrounding the town and he would judge which fancy dress was the best. There was to be a competition for adults and one for children in each village. The winners would be given a voucher to visit the cinema in town every week for a year. It was a fantastic prize and of course everybody wanted to win it !

Pinky just didn't have a clue what to wear ! She went next door to Queenie's house to see if she had any ideas of what she could wear. Queenie had already decided that she was going dressed as a sweep. She had bought a spiky wig and poked an old jacket and trousers up the chimney in her sitting room so that they were covered with soot. She fetched a couple of long handled brushes from her broom cupboard to show Pinky and they were covered in soot as well.

'I'm going to rub soot on my face as well on the competition day,' she said to Pinky. 'Then I will really look like a sweep won't I?' Pinky agreed it was a good idea but what was Pinky to wear? Everything that Queenie suggested, Pinky didn't like the idea.

'What about a cowgirl?' suggested Queenie. 'I know somebody who is going as a cowboy so you could go as a pair, couldn't you?'

'Oh no !' groaned Pinky. 'What with my legs ! I don't think so. It's not a knobbly knee competition you know !'

'Oh all right !' grumbled Queenie. 'Well what about going as a sunflower? I've got lots growing in my garden. I could make you a hat and a dress and stick sunflower petals all over them if you like.'

'No, I don't think so. Knowing my luck the petals will all shrivel on the day and I will look more like a rain flower,' replied Pinky gloomily. 'It's all right I will think of something, I just don't know what that will be yet,' and shaking her head, Pinky went back to her shop.

All that day and for the rest of the week, all Pinky's customers could talk about was the fancy dress competition. Pinky heard about lots of costumes that her customers and their children were going to wear. Someone was going as a ghost and there would be a ballet dancer, a pirate, an aeroplane pilot, then lots of sorts of heroes such as Superman. Superwoman, Bat Man, Spiderman and Captain America. But it was no good, Pinky just couldn't think of anything she could dress up as. She wanted to wear something unusual, but what? She thought about things to do with nature. What about a snowman? But no, someone else had already taken that idea.

In the end, Pinky just gave up and decided just to go and help the people setting up the stage on the village green instead. She tied some balloons in batches along the front of the stage and pinned them to the colourful streamers that were already pinned there. Then, she helped the head of the village committee Mrs Sproggins to put up a colourful banner along the top of the stage which said Robindale Village Fancy Dress Competition. When all the chairs were put up in front of the stage there was nothing else to be done so Pinky went home, tired but excited. Tomorrow would be the day of the competition and she just couldn't wait for it to come !

On Saturday morning, Pinky dressed herself with care as she was to help the competitors on and off the stage and she wanted to look her best. She put on a pink frilly blouse and a pink skirt which was covered in white bobbles. The blouse had 'Oh I do like to be beside the seaside,' written across the front of it and she had bought it when she had stayed at the seaside with her friend Izzy. Just for fun, she put on a bright pink wig which was fashioned into a beehive shape. Then she called for Queenie and the two friends made their way across the village green to where the competition was taking place.

The first competition was the children's fancy dress. Pinky and Queenie thought some of the children looked amazing ! There were children dressed as fairies, firemen, nurses, postmen, hot dogs, carrots, pumpkins and tomatoes. In fact, quite a lot of the children dressed up as items of food. As promised, Pinky helped them up onto the stage and then down the steps at the other end. Then she and Mrs. Sproggins stood at both ends of the line up of competitors while the mayor made his decision.

'The winner of the children's competition is....', the mayor paused and looked at the expectant faces of the children. 'It's Billy Brebner who is dressed as a tin of baked beans. Well done Billy ! Here is your prize.' Then, the mayor presented Billy with a cinema voucher which he could use every week for a year.

'Oh well done Billy !' Pinky whispered to him as she helped him down the stairs of the stage. His proud Mum and Dad stood by the steps waiting for him and they gave him a big hug

'Gosh, I can't believe that I've won !' Billy said as he and his family walked back to their seats amid the cheers and pats on his baked beans outfit that he got from his neighbours.

'Now, for the grown-ups competition.' announced Mrs. Sproggins. 'Please line up and then come onto the stage one by one so we can have a good look at you all.'

There were certainly some weird and wonderful fancy dress outfits in the grown-ups competition. There were jungle explorers, detectives, policemen, T.V characters like Marge Simpson and film characters like Shrek. Pinky helped them all to go onto the stage and off it again. Once again the competitors lined up again to await the mayor's decision while Mrs. Sproggins and Pinky stood at each end.

'The winner is...' the mayor paused to keep

everybody in suspense. 'It's Pinky Spinks who is dressed as pink and white candy floss.'

Pinky gasped ! 'Candy floss ! I don't look like candy floss, do I ? Surely it must be a mistake !'

'Well, the mayor thinks you do, Pinky. You mustn't embarrass the mayor and refuse the prize. After all you did send in an entry form so he probably thought you were in the competition.' said Mrs. Sproggins.

Pinky felt embarrassed because what she had put on was just a normal outfit for her except for the pink wig. The fact that she had put on the blouse about the sea side was just a coincidence ! But everybody in the audience was clapping and cheering. So, she went up to the mayor to receive her prize and then walked off the stage. All her friends and neighbours crowded around her to congratulate her.

PINKY HADN'T EVEN TRIED TO WIN THE PRIZE BUT SHE HAD TRIUMPHED IN THE END JUST LIKE SHE ALWAYS DID !

THE END

Printed in Poland
by Amazon Fulfillment
Poland Sp. z o.o., Wrocław